I know a lot of things

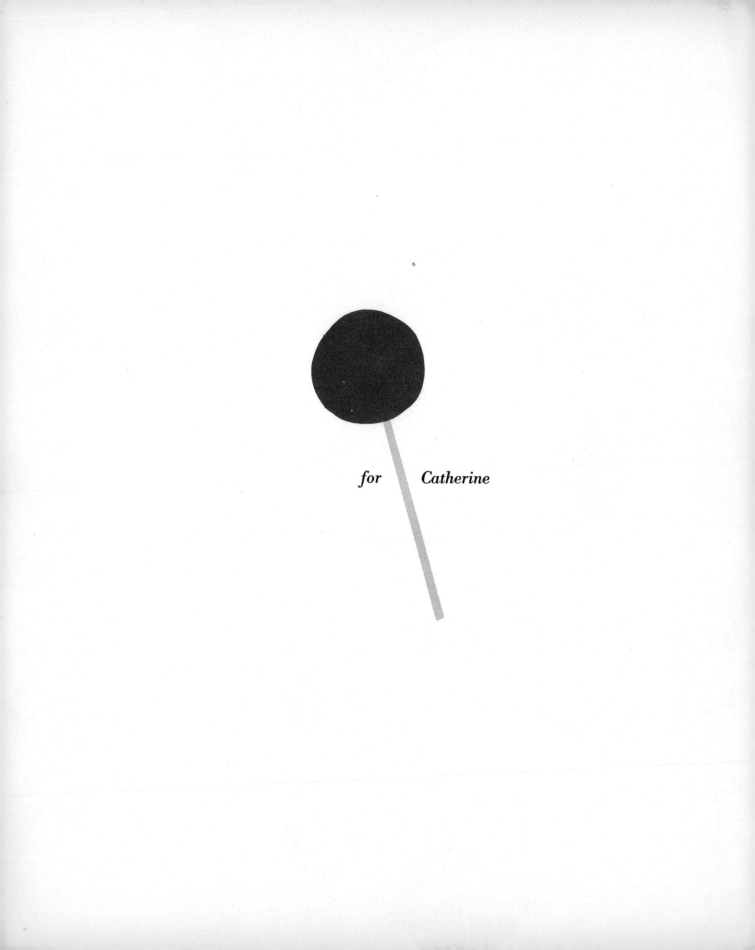

for   *Catherine*

I know
a lot
of
things

by Ann & Paul Rand

*Harcourt, Brace
and Company,
New York*

I know such a lot of things...
I know when I look
in a mirror
what I see is me.

I know a cat goes meow

a dog goes bowwow
and that is how
they talk.

Of course I know
a horse can pull
a wagon full
of wood.

And even an ant
could carry
a load on his back
big as a berry

and a leaf be a ferry
for a snail.

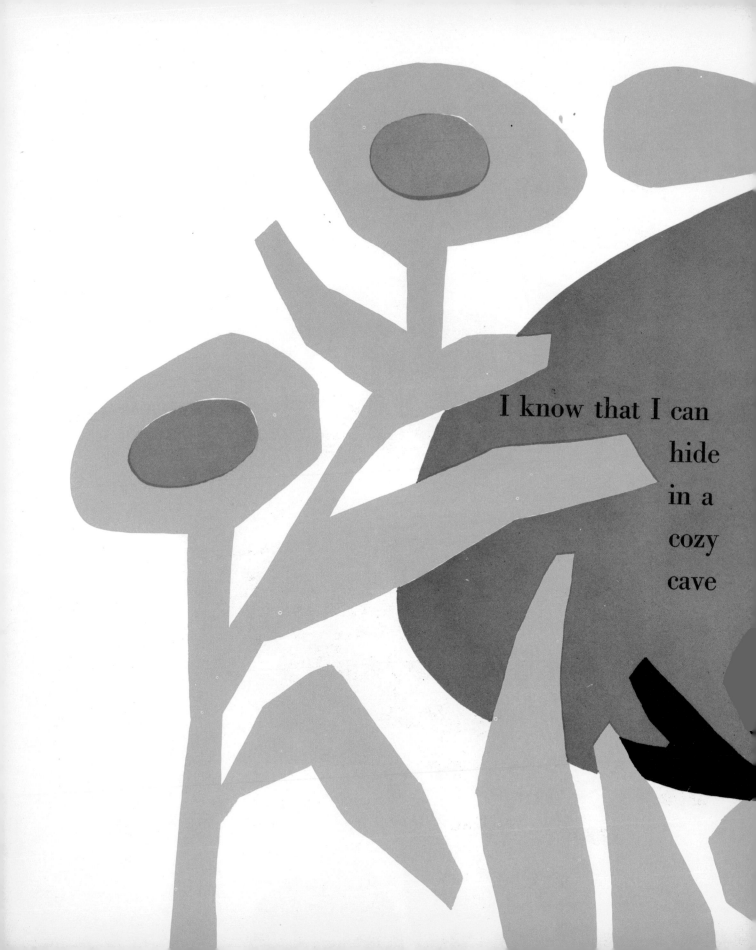

I know that I can
hide
in a
cozy
cave

or ride a big blue wave

across the sea.

I know I can dig

a hole this big

and climb a tree
high as the sky
to watch a bird fly by
and an acorn drop
kerplop kerplop

or wave hello   to a mushroom

who's just a little fellow with a big umbrella.

I know how things are made.
A house has glass
and bricks
and lots of sticks.
A square box has
a top as wide
as its side.

A book needs pages
and a cake
takes
ages
to bake.

I know the world is wide,
and a star
is far away,
and the moon is a light
for the night,
and the sun
is round as a bun
and very bright.

Oh

I know

such

a

lot

of

things,

but

as

I

grow

I know

I'll

know

much

more.